Loose Laces

by
Professer Clickity Klunk

Illustrated by
Gerald W. Tisdale

Published by

**DOWN THE PATH
PUBLISHING**

First Edition

Published in Canada 2011
By Down the Path Publishing
PO Box 344, Clearwater B.C. V0E 1N0

Email:
books@ProfesserKlunk.com
David@DownThePathPublishing.com
Printed in China
Library and Archives Canada Cataloguing in Publication

Klunk, Clickity, 1955-
Loose laces / by Professer Klunk ; illustrations by Gerald W.
Tisdale. -- 1st ed.

(A cautionary tale by Professer Klunk)
Issued also in mini softcover format.
ISBN 978-0-9865417-5-9

I. Tisdale, Gerald W. II. Title. III. Series: Klunk, Clickity, 1955- .
Cautionary tale.

PS8621.L856L66 2011 jC811'.6 C2011-905106-0

Loose Laces

Now this is a story

About a young boy who

Never, would ever

Would lace up his shoe.

One he would tie

But the other he'd say

"Never, not ever

Shall I lace up, no way."

Sometimes the cat

Would chase after that lace

He would then laughing

Turn red in the face.

Catching his breath

Again he would say

"Never, not ever

Shall I lace up no way."

One day in the winter

He had a challenge to face

The ground at the bus stop

Froze fast to his lace.

Putting salt from his pocket

To his lace on the ground

He was free to catch the next bus

The next bus that came around.

Smiling and laughing

Again he did say

"Never, not ever

Shall I lace up, no way."

Sometimes he would trip

Sometimes he would stumble

Sometimes down the stairs

Sometimes he would tumble.

At the bottom of the stairs

Again he would say

"Never not ever

Shall I lace up, no way."

His Dad said "Come here,

See here's what I do;

You can see how one bow

Gets tied on each shoe."

To which he said "Dad,

Here's what I know

Last time I laced both shoes

There was only one bow!"

Then away he did scamper

And again he did say

"Never, not ever

Shall I lace up, no way."

His mother she thought

About what she could do

About her little boy

Who laced only one shoe.

When at the shoe store

She remembered his song

Bought him shoes without laces

The ones that slip on.

So ends this story

When again he did say

"Never, not ever

Shall I lace up, no way."

About the Artist

Gerald W. Tisdale
Cartoonist.

Residing in Clearwater British Columbia, Gerald is the creator of "TisToons." His whity cartoons have been publilished in numerous papers through out B.C. for over twenty years and

Photo by Sherry Tisdale

currently published in the North Thompson Times. Gerald placed in the top three finalists for cartoon category in the British Columbia and Yukon Community Newspaper Association 2010 Ma Murray Awards. Loose Laces is the second Professer Clickity Klunk book, Gerald has illustrated.

Proofread by Helen Moller

Other Books by Professer Klunk

Andrew's Monster
Emily Car
Her Beef Stew
Horace the Cat
Puppy Named Rufus
Sammy's Gas
Wishfilled Thinking
Whoa There Now Nelly

Andrew's Mini
Emily Car Mini
Her Stew Mini
Horace Mini
Loose Laces Mini
Rufus Mini
Sammy's Gas Mini
Wishfilled Mini
Whoa Nelly Mini

DOWN THE PATH
PUBLISHING

www.ProfesserKlunk.com
books@professerklunk.com

Photo by Lemmikki Teder

Professer Klunk has been creating Cautionary Tales since the last century, reading to the delight of school children and teachers from The Eastern Townships of Quebec through Manitoba to the Islands and Towns of British Columbia.

Below are some parents comments...

Our son won't let go of you book, he sleeps with it and eats with it.

Your stories are the only ones my children want at bedtime now.

We have been looking for your books ever since my sister bought one in Georgetown.

Here's what some children said...

I liked your poetry because it has humor in it.

Thank you for making me feel more good about poetry.

I like all of your books they are really good, we loved them so much.

DOWN THE PATH PUBLISHING

$7.99

ISBN 978-0-9865417-5-9

60799

9 780986 541759